ONE PIG
WENT FOR A DRIVE

For Oliver Persaud and Sam Gurney Griffiths
oink oink! ~ A.D.

For Beatrice Quinney ~ T.F.

First published 2009 by Macmillan Children's Books
a division of Macmillan Publishers Limited
20 New Wharf Road, London N1 9RR
Basingstoke and Oxford
Associated companies throughout the world
www.panmacmillan.com

ISBN: 978-1-4050-2206-4 (hb)
ISBN: 978-1-4050-2207-1 (pb)

Text copyright © Alan Durant 2009
Illustrations copyright © Tor Freeman 2009
Moral rights asserted

1 3 5 7 9 8 6 4 2

A CIP catalogue record for this book is available from the British Library.

Printed in Belgium

ALAN DURANT

ONE PIG
WENT FOR A DRIVE

ILLUSTRATED BY TOR FREEMAN

MACMILLAN CHILDREN'S BOOKS

One pig went for a drive.

He went for a drive in his motor car.

When . . .

TOWN
5 MILES

SpLUTTER   SpLUTTER

SPLOT

The engine stopped.

"Excuse me," said Harry to a
passing pig, "can you help?"

And she could.
It was Myrtle, a pig with puff.

She huffed and she puffed
and she pushed that car to the
top of the hill until, at last . . .

. . . it started!

"Thank you," said Harry. "Are you going far?"
"I'm going to town," said Myrtle.
"Hop in," said Harry. "I'll give you a lift
in my motor car."

Two pigs went for a drive.

They went for a drive in a motor car.

When . . .

BUMPETY

BUMPETY

BUMPETY

FLUMP

A tyre went flat.

"Excuse me," said Harry to a passing pig, "can you help?"

And he could.
It was Percy, the mechanic,
with his box of tools.

He took off the tyre and he put on another.
Now that car was ready to roll again!

"Thank you," said Harry.
"Are you going far?"

"I'm going to town," said Percy.
"Hop in," said Harry. "I'll give
you a lift in my motor car."

Three pigs went for a drive.

They went for a drive in a motor car.

When . . .

SSSSSSSSSSSSSSSSSS

The radiator started to steam.

"Excuse me," said Harry to a passing pig, "can you help?"

And she could.

It was Winnie with her watering can.

She filled the radiator with water.

"Thank you," said Harry. "Are you going far?"
"I'm going to town," said Winnie.
"Hop in," said Harry. "I'll give you a lift
in my motor car."

Four pigs went for a drive.

They went for a drive in a motor car.

When . . .

WHEEE

SCREECH

BONK

The car skidded and swerved . . .

. . . right off the road.

"Excuse me," said Harry to a
passing pig, "can you help?"

And he could.

It was Sam, the strongman.
He heaved and he hoved,

he strained and he groaned,

and he got that car
on the road again.

"Thank you," said Harry. "Are you going far?"
"I'm going to the circus at the edge of town,"
said Sam.

"Hop in," said Harry. "I'll give
you a lift in my motor car."

Five pigs went for a drive.
They went for a drive in a
motor car.

They shouted and they sang
and they honked the horn.

When . . .

TOWN
1 MILE

CRASH

BASH

BING

BANG

CLANGA

LANGA

CLUNK

"Excuse me," said Harry to his passenger pigs. "Can anybody help?"

But no one could.

Not Sam the strongman.

Not Winnie with her watering can.

Not Percy the mechanic with his box of tools.

Not Myrtle with all her puff.

No one could put Harry's motor car together again.

"Oh dear," said Harry. "I cannot give you a lift to town."

"Don't worry," said Sam. "We're nearly there now.
Why don't you come to the circus with me?
Be my guests. See the show for free!"

So five pigs gave up driving.
They gave up driving in that motor car
and they went to the circus instead.

And after the show,
when it was time to go,

one pig went for a ride.
He went for a ride on a unicycle . . .

. . . all the way home!